Clint Faraday
54
Death From Natural Causes

Clint receives a call from Rico Hernandez, police, The Darien. He says Dave said to call. There is a body of a man known to hang around with drug dealers and mafia types.

"How was he killed?"

"Tortured several ways, then executed. It's what I want to call natural causes."

"Natural causes?"

"The people he was involved with? Torture and execution are natural causes!"

Clint Faraday
54
Death From Natural Causes
© 2019 by C. D. Moulton

Contents

About the author

CD Moulton has traveled extensively over much of the world both in the music business, where he was a rock guitarist, songwriter and arranger and in an import/export business. He has been everything from a bar owner to auto salvage (junkyard) manager, longshoreman to high steel worker, orchid grower to landscaper, tropical fish farmer to commercial fisherman. He started writing books in 1983 and has published more than 350 books as of January 1, 2023. His most popular books to date are about research with orchids, though much of his science fiction and fantasy work has proven popular. He wrote the CD Grimes, PI series, and the Det. Nick Storie series, Clint Faraday series, and many other works.

He now resides in Gualaca, Chiriqui, Panamá, where he writes books, plays music with friends, does research with orchids and medicinal plants. He has lately become involved in fighting for the rights of the indigenous people, who are among his closest friends, and in fighting the extreme corruption in the courts and police in Panamá.

He offers the free e-book, *Fading Paradise*, that explains what he has been through because of the corruption.

CD is the discoverer of the Chadam Protocol for curing cancer.

Facebook page Ambrosia peruviana for cancer.

Clint Faraday, retired detective from Florida, now living on the comarca Ngobe Bugle, Panamá, with his beautiful young wife and two teenage children (he was declared Ngobe by the council, a fact of which he was very proud), sighed and looked out over the water of the Caribbean.

He was, at present, living in his home near Cusapín. His wife, Tyna, was with his daughter, Nicole(13), in Cusapín to help with the cooking for the people. They worked there every third day.

Nito (Clintonito – 14) was out with Omar getting lobster and conch. Clint had spent the morning clearing the ground for planting frijoles.

Clint had millions of dollars he'd made through the detective work. He spent most of it building schools and clinics and such on the comarcas. He considered the Indigenos as being his people. The whole family work exactly as the other Indios worked. It is their place in the society.

In Indigeno society a person had a place, a purpose, responsibility to the community. That was what was sadly lacking in the world's major societies.

The cellular buzzed. It was Judi Lum, his neighbor when he was in Bocas del Toro. She chatted a bit about the projects and caught Clint up to date with what was happening. She said Dave, their nutty musician/botanist/ writer friend, had gone to The Darien a few days ago. They would probably not hear of him for awhile.

Dave was over eighty years old now. He still tramped around the jungles doing his botanical research, mostly with orchids.

After a few minutes of sorting through things at his desk the phone buzzed again.

"Mr. Clinton Faraday? I'm Enrique Hernandez, just Rico, with the National Police. I was asked by a friend of yours, a somewhat strange person called Dave, to call you about a body we found in the mountains."

"I'm just Clint. Dave *is* a strange person. I thought Dave was in The Darien somewhere wandering around the jungle. Where are you?"

"The Darien. He said to ask you to clear this up. He doesn't like the kind of people ... they are trouble."

"Tell me a short bit about it."

"A semi-local – by that, I mean he spent about half his time in the area – man called Tiburón, of what you would call shady character, was found, tortured and executed with a bullet in the back of the head near a path into the mountains. I want to call it natural causes, but Dave said it could get bad if it were allowed to continue."

"Natural causes?"

"The people he was involved with? – torture and execution are natural causes. They are people who were once with the drug cartels in Colombia who are, people will say, hiding here. Tiburón would tell who and where they are – for a price. It is just to shut him up, but your friend, Dave, says there's a lot more to it than that."

"I'll come I suppose. I'm not doing much now and I'm prone to getting bored with perfection. If Dave says it could get bad if those cruds aren't stopped I take it seriously. They aren't bringing in any drugs through the middle of The Darien. I would have to agree there's more.

"How will I find you in the Darien?"

"Come to a small place called Pucuro. It is very close to Colombia. I will arrange to have someone bring you over here. I work out of El Real at the request of the Kuna on this sort of thing."

"Ah, yes! The Darien is a comarca, actually, three of them.

"It will probably take me seven or eight hours to get there. It'll be at ... in the morning. I have a friend in Chiman I can stay with tonight."

"But ... It takes eleven hours on the bus to

Chiman from David. You will not arrive here until late tomorrow or early Friday!"

"I have a helicopter that can bring me. He has to come from David. We can be in Chiman tonight and he'll bring me there in the morning. I'll need the GPS coordinates."

"Great Gods of old! It will cost three or four thousand dollars to have a helicopter bring you here! The National Police can't afford that!"

"It's a service I use all the time. It doesn't cost the National Police anything. I'll see you in the morning."

The Trip

The chopper came about an hour later. Clint had gotten in touch with Tyna and told her he would be gone for a few days. A murder in The Darien.

"Dave is there. Why is there always a murder when he's somewhere?"

"No more than usual. The difference is that when he's there I get contacted."

They chatted for a few more minutes, then Clint took his backpack to the little sunny knoll by the vegetable garden to wait. The chopper came about ten minutes later and they were on their way. They landed in Chiman just as the light was fading. He and Pedro, the pilot/friend, had a good time talking with the natives and catching up on what was happening in the area.

In the morning at the first light they left for Pucuro. All they had was a map that showed it was really in the middle of nothing. They did have the GPS coordinates so could go directly there. They would stop in La Palma for fuel, then on to Pucuro. 3 – 4 hours.

They were flying over lush jungle and quite a number of rivers. The mountains were mostly under 1500 feet, but a few were as high as forty five hundred feet. Pucuro was at about 1200 feet so was probably a relatively comfortable place. The elevation dropped toward the Pacific, but rose toward the Caribbean.

They were about three quarters of an hour from Pucuro when Pedro got an emergency call to go to La Doncella. They were close. The chopper was needed to take two people to the hospital in El Real. That was on the way, but Clint would have to stay in La Doncella until Pedro could take the patients and return. There wasn't room in the chopper for three passengers.

Clint agreed to use of the chopper immediately. That took precedence over a murder somewhere. The murder victim was already far past being helped. It would mean about two hours delay, which wasn't critical to anything.

The patients were two people who were caught in a house fire and were badly burned. Fast care would save them and would result, with the combination of natural medicines, to see that scarring wasn't too bad.

The people were dirt poor. They couldn't afford any helicopter ambulance!

Pedro said there would be no charge about the same time Clint said he would pay all expenses, including the patients' return to the town when they were treated and could travel.

La Doncella was a typical little settlement. The people were Indio to the greatest extent.

Clint asked about the fire. No one could explain how it happened. No one in the house smoked, there was no electricity to cause a fire. The cooking was on a wood stove under a thatched roof hut. The fire was in the house, not from there.

Clint saw the victims. One woman of about forty five years and one about twenty two or three. The local medicine woman had sedated them, so they couldn't talk.

It didn't look right to Clint. He would be there for about two hours so he would try to find what had happened – and who set that fire. It had started in the sala in the cloth from the drapes over the front window and had spread rapidly to a sofa, which released the gases that quickly resulted in the women becoming unconscious.

How had the fire gotten into the bedroom? There was no connection Clint could see, but it seemed that it had jumped from the sala to the bedroom, about twelve feet, where it caught the clothes on the rack by the bed on fire, then it caught the mattress.

A neighbor saw the fire and called for help. The bed was burning, but the women weren't in the direct fire yet. They would have been in a minute or less!

The neighbor threw a bucket of water on the bed and another ran in to help pull the women from the bed. They were burned, mostly first degree burns, but some second degree. The main danger was that they had inhaled some very dangerous fumes from that sofa.

Clint went to the little cantina and talked with the neighbor, who said Janeta, the older woman, had lost her husband four years ago. Ilena, the daughter, was popular, but didn't want to get serious with anyone yet. There was some trouble from two or three men who wanted her. Joel Enrique and Carlos Flores were the worst. They wouldn't leave her alone. The police were called a couple of times when they fought each other over her. She said she wouldn't have either of them, so they were crazy.

Juanita, the woman who ran the café, said Janeta said her daughter was dating a man from Yaviza. A man with a job and a man with some education and culture. She had just announced that three days ago.

Janeta and Ilena were very well-liked in the community. No one would want to harm them

Clint thought, then decided to find where Flores and Enrique were last night. He asked around. Enrique was staying out of town on a finca to watch the place while the owner was in El Real. He couldn't have been in La Doncella last night.

Flores was around town. He was at the Cantina Pajaro at about eleven, when it closed.

There was one police officer in town. Clint found him in the café and introduced himself. Jaime Geraldo, the officer, had heard of him.

"Do you know where we can find this Carlos Flores now?"

"Flores? Probably in the square."

"Shall we go arrest him for attempted murder?"

"I wouldn't be surprised, but are you serious?"

"Yes. The two women who were burned. He set the fires."

"Fires?"

"The drapes that released toxic fumes to, as we say, render the victims unconscious and the one in the bedroom after they were thus rendered."

"If you can give me motive, he was the only one here – well, Enrique, but he's not in town.

"You see, I am suspicious, but he wanted to marry Ilena the same as ten others of us. He would not harm her, I think."

"Janeta announced a couple of days ago that Ilena is seriously considering marriage with a man in Yaviza."

"Yaviza? Morales? He is the kind of person she would find suitable, I believe. I had not heard that, but why would ...? Because of the old, old thing. 'If I can't have her, nobody can!'

"That is motive. It is now for him to disprove it. I think he can't! He had fights on three occasions with Enrique over her. She was not interested in either and said they were crazy to fight over her when she wouldn't have either."

"You would have found about the announcement and would have solved it."

"Yes, but this makes it faster and easier. I think we are much alike in our processes of proving a thing."

"I hear Pedro coming back. It passed the time while I waited."

Jaime laughed. "You will go to Pucuro and I will arrest a would-be killer. We each have our duties!"

Clint waved and headed for the little field where Pedro was just settling. He got aboard and they were on their way again.

The rest of the way was over lush jungle. It was truly beautiful. Pucuro was another small town much like La Doncella.

Rico met the chopper and said he had arranged for Clint to stay with some people there. Very few people other than Indios came to purcuro.

"I'm Ngobe, but that's not important. Tiburón was Indio?"

"Mestizo. He and that Russian fellow, Viktor – *Mr.* Ivanovich – and a gringo named Clancy and a Colombian named Mendez were the only non-natives here. There are a few others within a few kilometers who are not Indio. It makes it clear that one of them killed him. No one here would have any reason. It isn't the affair of this place, but perhaps Dave is right that it could bring more of the type here. We do not need nor want that!"

"No. You certainly don't need any Russian Mafia here. I've heard of Ivanovich. I have to agree there's something up that could get very hairy!"

Clint had one thing he would do the minute he suspected that the so-called Russian mafia were involved with anything. He made a phone call.

"Mikail? Clint Faraday here. How are things with you and the family? Well, I hope."

"Ah! Clinton! We are much better than we have a right to be, my friend. Ilya is going to attend the university in Moscow. It is well I have all my ill-gotten gains. I could not otherwise afford such extravagances!

"How is the beautiful wife and family? Living in your paradise and prospering? Do you still insist in doing that hard labor when you could afford to hire everyone on the comarca to do it for you?" He laughed.

"Yep! The whole family is enjoying their place in our society.

"We have one, Mikail. You and your two kids have no place where they belong. They spend their lives looking for a place." They had this discussion many times in the past.

"Ah! My dear friend, I say again that you are correct. You have a place among many people, I am just some rich crook among many millions more rich crooks. It is what I know.

"This locator thing on the telephone tells me you are in The Darien? Have you found more stolen atomic bombs there?"

"No, and I don't ever need to get involved in that idiocy again, thank you!

"Mikail, what do you know about a man named Viktor Ivanovich?"

There was a lasting silence. Clint waited.

"Clint ... Ivanovich disappeared and is thought by interested parties to be dead. He was in Colombia with an Irishman named Clancy James. They were dealing with a man from the cartel called simply 'The Shark' in Cali. They have discovered something. It is bigger than a few billion dollars worth of drugs. We do not know what it is, but it involves a group of German scientists who fled to South America at the end of the war.

"I cannot tell you what is involved. I can only say that I was part of a conversation, not yet a year ago, where a scientist from Sweden stated that a theory may be far from truth, but may, in some cases, lead to results that – I am messing it up – she said that a theory my be incorrect, but may have a significant part that leads to a theory that does work.

"I am trying to translate from Swedish. I think you can understand the idea that lies behind the statement.

"I remember! Dr. Bergman said it well! He said, 'Because a theory is wrong does not mean that it doesn't work! If it seems to work one may build a better theory from it!'

"They were medical research scientists I think. Genetic researchers. Dr. Bergman was deep into stem cell science.

"Clint, maybe they have found the cure for cancer? Maybe AIDS?"

"Wouldn't they want that known?"

"In some cases, no. I must check some sources. I may assume that Viktor is not dead. That is information I will keep below the desktop until I learn the significance. I would know what is of major importance with this.

"I will not betray word of this. Is Viktor alone involved with you there?"

"I haven't met the, er, gentleman. He's here with Clancy and a Colombian named Renaldo Mendez. Tiburón is the body."

"I see. I think it is unlikely that any of them killed any other of them, thus someone else is there. From the station relay from which you emanate you are at the limit of population near Colombia.

"Clinton, those are the people you speak of as 'your' people. One thing of which you can be absolutely certain is that those foreigners and the one or ones who are there after them are as dangerous as any of which you have ever had knowledge. I think they will not want publicity that would result from any attack on the general people there, but that does not include you. Take the very greatest care, my friend."

"That, I can promise you! Thanks, Mikail."

"De nada." He rang off.

Clint sat back to think, then called Manny Mathews, a friend with connections all over the world. He didn't have a hint.

He called Basilio on the comarca near his family and asked that he quietly see that no one gets near his family. That would be a sure thing!

He called Judi Lum, his neighbor in Bocas Town, to have her keep her ears open about anything concerning the Russian mafia and any connections to drug cartels and medicine. Judi was a genius at getting information in unexpected ways.

"Drugs, Russians and medicine? Weird.

"I've heard a few little things about somebody in the Medellin area who found something that keeps him from getting older. He's supposed to have spent a hundred million dollars to have aging stopped. It seemed to be working. He was in his eighties and looks like he's forty. He actually looks younger than he did five years ago when Julio visited. He looked about fifty five then!

"Julio is Julio Esteves. He's related to some Indios in that part of Colombia who work for the cartels. His friend is sort of a valet to Eschevaria. He's right there in the house and says he sees the old turkey getting younger and younger. Some German doctor who claims to be a hundred twenty five years old comes every month to give him injections. The doctor looks like he's thirty, according to Julio.

"I thought it was just one of the ten thousand stories going around. It is, isn't it?"

"Judi, I'm a long way from sure of anything!"

They chatted, then Clint immediately called Mikail.

"Mikail? Clint. Life extension?"

"Name."

"Eschevaria."

"Doctor?"

"German is all I know. A hundred twenty five."

"So. How much did Benicio pay?"

"Skinny is a hundred mil. Yun."

"I have reports that Benicio Exchevaria has gone from eighty seven to thirty five over a period of six years. His doctor is Hans Goerher, a research doctor for Hitler. He is a hundred forty two years old, going on thirty."

"Mikail, if they have something like that they could let it be known that you can lose, say, fifty years for a hundred million, cash. They would have more money than has ever been printed or minted in a year! What's going on?"

"Philosophy, much of which I can offer no refutation. A hundred million will allow them to live another century or two in comfort.

"Dr. Goerher is a Malthusian. That should tell you why it isn't known. Within a couple of years there would be generic crap on TV claiming that for a mere five thousand dollars you could be guaranteed to look and feel twenty five years younger! With this offer you also receive Dr. Goerher's own special formula aloe skin cream. That is a fifty dollar value in itself! Call now! This is a limited offer!"

"And the population would rise faster than it is anyhow. It's already a long way past ridiculous.

"It seems strange that a researcher under Hitler would care about that."

"Hitler funded those scientists. A hell of a lot of them really didn't know what was happening outside of their laboratories.

"Goerher was into advanced research. DNA and genetic science and stem cell science and ten more came together. He had a way to stop aging, it is rumored, in the seventies. It seems he has found the way to reverse it.

"I think I do not want to live to be a hundred fifty, though knowing one might be in perfect health for that entire time would tend to make a difference."

"I think I have to find who's here and what the murder was about, but only to make it damned plain that life extension isn't worth shit if your head's chopped off with a machete!"

"That would seem to be a truth to consider! A bullet through a hundred year old head that looks like only a thirty year old head results in life extension termination in a rather definite way!"

They chatted a few more minutes, then Clint called Tyna and chatted about things for almost an hour. Things were normal on the comarca.

Now to find who was there who was not from the area. He found Rico and said they had to find who killed Tiburón and had to send a message out with them.

"Rico, killing him wouldn't prove anything. They have to kill them all. You don't know what this kind of thing can bring. It'll be hell if whoever killed him knows about ... certain things a drug lord is into."

"I cannot figure what a drug lord wants here.

There is absolutely no reasonable way to bring drugs through many miles of dense jungle to a place like this where there would be no way to transport them farther."

"It's about a drug lord, not about drugs. In fact, drugs have no consideration in this, other than the profits from a long time ago are what they're operating under. The drugs just happened to be there in the past. They paid for something else."

"I was told by three friends who have worked with you that you seldom make sense, but you always get results."

Clint gave him the finger. "Where can I find Clancy, Mendez and Ivanovich?"

"They are said to be going to La Palma."

"But?"

"Your friend, Dave, is between El Naranjal and Paya on the Rio Paya."

"They're with him?!"

"I don't have solid evidence."

Clint thought about it. He walked around the little village with Rico awhile, then went to the place he was staying. He dug out a throwaway phone and called a number only he, Judi and Manny knew. Dave answered immediately.

"I've been waiting for you to call. I left them in El Naranjal with some friends. I don't know if I agree with them, but can't refute their argument.

Sharky ran his mouth and they knew he would bring some dangerous things down on himself. There will be Indios from Colombia looking for us. I don't think they can blend with the people here enough to fool many. They'll claim to be Kuna, which they could get by with.

"Don't say anything. Clancy says they have sophisticated transmitters. They'll know where to plant them if you've been there more than half an hour.

"This is about something I find hard to believe, but I've seen the evidence. I've got copies of photographs for ten years that, when you lay them out, look like one of those films you run in reverse. Maybe you already know what I'm talking about. Look into life extension.

"I'll text the GPS location where you can find them. Maybe you can find a way to get them somewhere they can hope to live more than a few more hours.

"I'm going on down the river. I'm not getting any younger – which is what this is about – and would like to finish a little more of this research.

"Clint, be damned careful! They can use a blow-gun and drop you with curare. Fast, silent, and damned efficient.

"Got to go. Get the GPS info and break the chip. They're more up on that kind of shit than the FBI or CIA – which isn't saying a hell of a lot.

"Caio!" He rang off. A minute later the text message tone rang. He memorized the numbers and took out the chip to smash with a rock on the terrace. He then tossed the pieces into the little stream and put a backup chip in the phone.

He used his regular cellular to call Pedro. He said to come get him. He used a code to say to bring the larger chopper and said he wasn't much interested in this kind of thing. It involved the Russian mafia so they weren't going to solve anything anyhow.

He went to find Rico. They talked a bit and walked along to stand beside a small, but loud, cascada for a minute. It was perfect white sound. He explained to Rico what he was doing as quickly as he could, then they strolled back into the village talking about the way Dave tramped through the jungles at his age.

Pedro came in about an hour and a half. Clint met him and they were soon rising and heading for La Palma. When they were out of sight of Purcuro, Clint gave Pedro the GPS coordinates and said, "I hope this thing's got plenty of fuel!"

They landed at the coordinates. It was a little meadow close to the Rio Paya. There was no evidence anyone was within fifty miles. Pedro shrugged. Clint said he was going to stroll around a bit and went toward the river. A big man with reddish curly hair stepped out from the jungle with an AK-47 pointed right between Clint's eyes.

"Clancy? I'm Clint."

He lowered the gun and sighed. "If it was them, this thing wouldn't prove anything. Dave says if anyone alive can get us out of here, it's you."

"We can give it a shot. If they came up with a hundred million for the process they can damned well spend a percent of that to keep it."

Clancy whistled and Mendez and Ivanovich soon came to go to the chopper. They had their tent and equipment in a large duffel-type bag they threw into the back and they all got in.

"Will this thing make Curacao?" Clint asked.

"Yeah."

"No!" Ivanovich cried. "They have people there!"

Clint thought, then went through some papers.

He used the radio to call Manny, who made some arrangements.

"David," Clint said. Pedro grinned and headed for David. He stopped at La Palma for three minutes, then they headed on. Clint made a call and told Pedro the coordinates of his friend near Calderas. They would stop there for no more than one short minute, then go on to David. Clancy, Ivanovich and Mendez would not be aboard when they landed in David.

That was almost three hours from now so they would discuss what was going on. Clint was curious.

"I suppose I know as much about them as anyone here," Ivanovich said. "It started in forty two. There were a number of people in science who fled Germany to South America.

"The most important here is Dr. Hans Goerher, who you have probably never heard of.

"Hans was working on a science project for the fuhrer. Extending the life of the fathers of his super race, basically. What was known of genetic science at the time was little as compared with today.

"Goerher is a genius. He was some years ahead of the field then. He had anticipated Watson and Crick in one area. He had actually made a gene insert in some plant or other in forty one! He produced a plant that used some genes from *amaranthus* that would produce a grain high in usable protein, as I understand it. *Amaranthus* produces protein, but this was a grain that produced more and better or something. It was hard to grow, but the insert worked. The process was lost when he fled Germany to Argentina, then moved to Venezuela, then Peru, then Colombia. He became involved with a man called Echevaria, who you may have heard of in the drug production area.

"Echevaria financed a few million dollars worth of laboratory equipment and worked alone on his project. He was twenty six years old in forty two. It was now two thousand. He was seventy four and looked it for the most part.

"In twenty oh eight he looked perhaps fifty or fifty five. He announced, only to Echevaria, that he had made the breakthrough. Something from what they call stem cells. He said he would use the process on Echevaria and only Echevaria. He would not extend life for any of the other thugs and crooks and the billions of people with no redeeming features about them. The world had far too many of those now.

"The entire project had cost Echevaria a little more than ten million at the time. Goerher said he could do his work and live for perhaps three hundred fifty years on one hundred million dollars. Take it or leave it.

"I was a laboratory assistant, of sorts, starting in twenty oh six. I did not know the science, but I knew the equipment. I was raised not far from Moscow. I studied organic chemical engineering and was considered bright. I was nineteen years old and had met a man called Generoso Batista on a vacation in Bogota. Everyone called him 'The Shark.' El Tiburón. He was known to be the favorite employee of a major drug lord named Echevaria. He was in Bogota at the university when we met. He was seeking a person to assist in a secret project.

"It took two days to convince me it was real, then I contacted Russia and said I was going to be in Colombia for a period of five years or more. I moved to the estate near Medellin and went to work. It was fascinating and the method was so far advanced over my education I could not believe it! I learned more in a few months than I could have learned at the university and was even moving ahead of what any professor there knew!

"I did a lot of the records work. I found the personal dossier of Dr. Goerher. It was amazing! He was born in nineteen twenty six! There were pictures of his youth, the kind of things that were saved then. Black and white photos, school pictures and so forth. He had garnered some awards in school, then there were pictures of him with Adolph Hitler and the entire Nazi Party elite!

The pictures showed him aging in a normal way until around nineteen eighty nine, when he seemed to stop aging at all, even to look a few years younger.

"I put it to makeup and perhaps plastic surgery and so forth – but there he was! He was about sixty years old, to look at!

"I found the picture record he had secreted in his study. He was growing steadily younger at perhaps triple the rate one ages.

"I gave Dave most of my pictures. Here is dated nineteen ninety. You can see that he was in his seventies and looked it."

Clint took the photo. It was a distinguished looking man who looked like Freud. The date was on the back. 5/Nov/ 99.

"Here is two thousand."

It was the same person. It looked like a picture taken three or four years earlier than the first. It was dated 17/May/00.

"Here is twenty oh one."

Even younger.

They went through the pictures, one each year, until twenty twelve. In twenty twelve Goerher looked like he was around thirty five.

"Here's Echevaria in twenty oh eight."

He looked like a typical Colombian higher class Latino. He was about seventy, Clint would guess.

"Here's two months ago.

"Four years? This much?"

He looked like maybe forty five.

"I saw that happening. Sharky saw it. Mendez saw it. Clance saw it.

"We were scared to the point of being terrified. A boy of sixteen years, an Indio who worked with the horses, told people in the village that Echevaria was getting younger and he had a couple of pictures proving it. He died a pretty horrible death. Everyone got the message.

"A sixteen year old kid, for God's sake! Christ! We were being watched. Echevaria hired only temporary help. Six months max. We had been there all along. It's like the mafia. You're in for life, like it or not!"

"Echevaria has fingers everywhere. We didn't know where to go. We grabbed an opportunity when there was a fire in a drug laboratory and everyone had to go help clean it up and hide the evidence. He and his goons were in the main lab, there was a Land Rover sitting right there. It would be at least two hours before he would know we were gone.

"We went. Mendez had been to Pucuro once and

said there was a good chance we could hide out there for awhile, then we could find another place.

"As you might have guessed, they found Sharky.

"We all carry some phony e-mail writeouts that suggest we're not together. I'm, according to the ISP code, in Costa Rica. Mendez is in Peru. Clance is in Mexico, heading for the states.

"We don't know which one or ones are Echevaria's goons. They are Indios who look much like the natives here. We have to disappear. We don't know how!"

"You're going to be dropped, almost literally, on an Indio friend's property. The chopper will go in, touch ground, you will jump, I'll toss out your bag and we'll go on. Anyone watching from where they can watch, even the satellites, won't believe we came in that close. No one can get there, I guarantee.

"I met a man who might have the perfect place to disappear – if I can convince him about this."

The discussed how the drop-off would work. The finca was the entire top of a mountain, very high, near Calderas. Clint and Judi had quite the adventure there! (Book 7 – *Comedy of Terrors*) It was in the comarca. The chopper would fly the valleys, not going to the top. It would be on the side of the mountain below the peak. Clint used his throwaway to call to say he was bringing the three.

Clint had the contacts to see when the four spy satellites used in close mapping and military intelligence (Yeah! Right!) would be east and couldn't see the side of the mountain for about ten minutes. They could be observed going behind the mountain and coming out the other side with so little time difference it wouldn't be noted.

It went off exactly! Pedro used acceleration behind the mountain to make it appear that they didn't pause anywhere for even that ten seconds. They were traveling at 120 and the anticipation circuits would say they moved at that speed and came out to the half second for if they simply were following a route at constant speed.

They landed in David. There were two cars by the fence at the chopper field to see them come in. Clint and Pedro got off the chopper. Clint took out his regular cellular and called Tyna to tell her he would be home soon. He had a couple hours work in David, then would be there. The code he used to tell her that (for others to hear) was that he didn't have a clue as to when he'd be home.

Had Alma called to say when she'd be there?

That told her he had to contact the famous detective in Florida, CD Grimes. She knew what he had to have.

"She called yesterday. She wants to know if you

can get in touch with Dave. I told her he was in The Darien and you had the way to contact him with your computer. She left their number ... where is it? I'll text it to you or something.

"Nito says for you to bring some Epsom salt when you come back, and some boric acid. The orchid plants Dave left need magnesium that the fertilizers here don't have. There are a lot of arieles (cutter ants) starting. We can get rid of them before there's a problem.

"Get some good cloth, that dark purple color, and some gold and bright green. Nito and Nicole need some new clothes.

"Nito's overdoing the sex bit. I guess that's natural at fourteen, but you have to talk to him. There's no problem here, but there's too much SIDA when we're on Bocas or in David.

"I miss holy hell out of you. I need the sex bit myself, you know!"

They teased and played a few minutes, then Clint rang off. His throwaway dinged with a text message that was CD Grimes' private number in Florida.

He called. A man Clint had talked with before, Tony Jacobi, answered and said to call a special number. It was direct to a satellite and no one could intercept it even if it didn't have a very complicated scrambled coding inserted.

Clint called the number with his throwaway. (He really would throw it away after this!)

CD wasn't available. He was in Europe. Tony handled things. CD had told Clint about that, so he asked if there was a way to get three people from Panamá to Kylvania (An island country off South America that the billionaire detective had bought and named after his computer genius). (CD Grimes, book 16 – *Deadly Island*) It was probably the most secure place in the world.

"CD told me about you. Nick Storie told me about you. Even Pancho told me about you. I won't ask questions.

"You say you have the use of a helicopter? Have the pilot call me and we'll set something up."

"He's right here. I can trust him."

Clint handed the phone to Pedro. He talked a few minutes, then said he'd make some kind of arrangements and call when he had it ready. It would be perfectly natural for a commercial helicopter company to come to Crane in Panamá City. After all, they built helicopters among the hundreds of other things they built.

Pedro soon hung up and told Clint it would be handled. He didn't need to know more. A man from Crane would contact him.

"Good enough! Take me to my family!"

Clint got off the chopper and Pedro took off. Tyna and the kids ran out to tackle him. They rolled around the grass and teased and played, then went to the house.

Clint explained about a lot of what had been happening. Tyna said Dave wanted him to call on the special phone CD Grimes had left. He was sure there was no way there was any audio there, but went a short distance into the forest to make the call.

"Clint, JK called and said he was expecting company on his island. He's down there at the moment. I told him about what I knew. He can check on anyone, anywhere. He said they're tied up with a drug lord named Echevaria who has grown forty years younger over the past ten years. Some doctor from Hitler's Germany is working on a fountain of youth thing that seems to work. The doctor lost fifty or more years.

"JK can't figure what the doctor wants. He would think the type would want all the money in the world – and he's in a position where he could damned well get it! He knows Echevaria's the type."

"Dr. Goerher's a Malthusian. He has a hundred million or so from Echevaria, who gets the treatments stopped if he tries any use that Goerher doesn't approve. Clancy, Viktor and Mendez are going to be smuggled to Kylvania. JK will love those pictures!

"I have to meet this JK character. CD and Alma said he could take over the world and never leave his little island. Maybe he could take over that part of the world and Pancho could take over the underworld."

"Neither one wants the responsibility.

"You going to drop it and let them live in their fantasy world?"

"No. Goerher killed a sixteen year old kid who had nothing to do with anything. I don't think he had a legitimate reason to kill Sharky and he doesn't have one to be going after Clancy and company. If he left other people alone, I'd say 'To hell with it!' He's not about to do that. He was with the Nazi scientists, so learned some techniques. He's not a nice person. Echevaria is no pillar of the community.

"What happens if Echevaria's treatments stop? He croaks?"

"He'll probably start aging again. Maybe at the four times rate."

They chatted a few minutes. Dave said to call JK and gave Clint the number. He did. He talked with the strange genius for more than an hour. JK was impressed with the method of using the internet to get information Clint had devised. He gave him a few pointers about getting other things and even gave him a code that would get him into Interpol and several other organizations in an untraceable manner.

Clint had some feelers out and would now play a waiting game. He also had a few traps set.

One thing was certain. If Echevaria or Goerher came after his family or friends there was going to be more hell for them to pay than they could conceive of!

"Clint? Pancho here. How are you and the family doing? Could you use a couple of visitors for a week or ten about now?"

Pancho was Pancho De Gulio, perhaps the most powerful person in the United States and several other countries where mobs and mafia were concerned. He wasn't part of them, but knew enough to destroy all of them with a word. His other detective friend from Florida, Det. Lt. Nick Storie, had introduced them and Pancho spent a week at Clint's Cusapín place two years before. He was personable and popular with the Ngobe.

"We'll expect you ... this afternoon?" Clint answered. "How are you, the wife and brat?"

"I will stay in David this evening and will come to Cusapín tomorrow afternoon if that is agreeable?"

"Jontoro! We'll have the guest room ready!"

Pancho laughed. The guest room was whatever space was available and they would sleep on mats on the floor, same as the Indios.

Pancho was probably a multi-billionaire, but was really a simple person. He was half Indio from Peru. He had to admit that sleeping on the mat left him feeling good when he got up. His back never hurt when he did that.

Clint could sleep in a hammock, but Pancho never could.

They chatted. Tyna came in and talked with Pancho and Gloria, Pancho's wife. They made plans to spend two days in Cusapín, go to the place in Quebrada Tula for three, then return to Cusapín. Gloria was Spanish, from Madrid, and the stay with Tyna and Clint before had been one of the most enjoyable in her life. She and Tyna were soul-mates in a lot of ways.

Clint took the phone again and told Pancho about the Echevaria thing. Pancho had discussed it with JK. Pancho said Echevaria was making some kind of plan. That was part of why he decided to visit Clint.

"I can make plans, too," Clint replied.

"As can I!"

"You want into that life extension thing?"

"No. Most definitely not. I'm not psychologically designed to live that long. I would keep such horrors from the hands of such garbage as Echevaria. If there were people who would be of value to the world who could handle it it could be a good thing.

"I think there is no one who is qualified to make those selections."

"Maybe Basilio?" The chief was just coming onto the porch. Clint handed him the phone and said it was Pancho, who he'd met (and Basilio had made a very strong positive impression on Pancho).

"Ah! Pancho! Coin dere! Clint had mentioned me?"

"I can think of no one."

"*ME?!* I would refuse. If it was forced on me, I would take any of a number of poisons."

"That is more than truth, my friend. Much more."

"Greed drives the world outside of the comarca. It is another greed where one doesn't stop to consider what he wants. He sees only the fantasy. Reality will, as Clint says, come to smack him in the puss, sooner or later."

"I will do that. You will always be a welcomed friend here. You and Nick are the only people I know who I would recommend for such a thing. And Clint and his family. The proof that I made a wise decision is that none of you would even consider it for a moment."

"I will do that. I can guarantee as much as it is possible to do so that they could not come here."

"Quebrada Tula? This place is ninety five percent secure while Quebrada Tula would be a hundred five percent. There is water to come here. Tula is in the mountains in the center of the comarca."

"I feel there is little danger. If Gloria has never been to such a place you will enjoy it greatly. I visit Clint when he is there."

"Yes. Life in paradise. Proof is that one thinks he would become bored, but that is easy to overcome. Each has a duty here. There is no time for boredom."

"I will. Tomorrow. I will roll out a palm frond in your honor – or something. Maybe." He laughed and handed Clint the phone. Clint talked a few more minutes, then rang off.

Nito came to hug Basilio and say that there was a boat just offshore. It came a couple of minutes ago and was just sitting there.

Clint grinned. He had done something that JK had suggested three days ago. Nito and Basilio grinned.

There was a metal screen hanging off the roof in front of the porch. It had a little motor with a ten-lobed cam that ran against the holder rod. The screen was electrified. The motor was solar powered. It vibrated and ran a phased electric current through the screen. Electronic listening devices would hear a lot of noise. Laser reflection would hear a very loud noise. Direct amplified sound would give them a lot of noise. Cameras would get a blur, even if they did have enough light behind the screen for a picture.

"Stupid!" Nito decided. "Mom says she has some fresh pineapple banana chicha if anyone wants any."

They went inside. Basilio said he hoped Nito had sense enough to not get Chacha pregnant. They were spending a lot of private time together lately.

"Dave has some stuff that's a hundred percent," Nito assured him.

They went inside joking about Nito's sexual exploits. Clint could just picture a father in the states joking about sex that way with as fourteen year old son. He could picture it never happening.

The rest of the day was spent doing the ordinary things on the comarca. Clint helped repair the tile roof on a local house and Tyna cooked for the workers' dinner. Nito and Nicole worked in the personal garden. They were tired and content when they went to bed.

Tomorrow morning Clint would finish the roof work. Tyna would wash clothes. Nito and Nicole would go to school.

Pancho, Gloria and Serena would come.

Eduardo and Omar, who did most of the fishing for the village, came to say there was a strange boat that kept coming back and forth. It spent a lot of time out from Clint's dock.

"Yeah. They're too stupid to know they're wasting a lot of fuel. They could just come in and you'd let them sit in the shade hut," Omar said. "I don't think I could do that. I'd get so bored from watching someone who didn't try to hide anything I'd probably try to see how deep I could go with a rock tied to my foot!"

Eduardo said they felt Clint should know the boat had three men who looked Indio, but who acted otherwise. They had some fancy things like Clint had shown them. Infra-red goggles and such silliness. With the moon so bright, who needed that crap?

They talked awhile, then left. Clint and Tyna went to bed.

Pancho and family were there two days. Nicole and Serena were great pals. Serena was thirteen. Nito was warned that she was off limits. She wasn't Ngobe, she was a gringa.

Tyna and Gloria were making plans to go to Quebrada Tula in the morning. Pancho was helping with gathering beans. Clint was cooking sugar.

Pancho fit very well. No one asked him to help with the village routine. He simply asked what he was to do and did it. Arnaldo was scheduled to work with the beans, but his mother's sister was in the hospital in Chiriqui Grande, so he went to her.

About eight o'clock Dave called on the special phone. Clint had carried it since the case started.

"Clint, I'm being followed. I'm in the middle of The Darien! It would have to be about that life extension thing."

"Are you safe enough?"

"Oh, no problem. The two guys with me know every move they make. They look like Indios, more like Cuna, but they don't act like them. Peco says they talk more Colombian. They would be from Echevaria. I don't have a clue what they want from me."

"They probably want to know where Viktor and company are and they want to know about any pictures or other things you may have."

"So? Ask me! I'll tell them those three are in Kylvania and that they have the pictures.

"How about I have Peco walk up to them and tell them that?"

"Only if you can be sure Peco would be safe doing it. It might work!"

"Peco will talk to them and I'll be with Reno in the jungle with them in the sights of a couple of three fifty sevens."

"Let me know what happens."

"I think maybe I'll talk to them with Peco and Reno having them in the sights. Might be fun!"

"Hay cuidado! This is no game!"

"It is to me. Maybe I'll conference with you on a call or I'll put this thing in my pocket. Turned on. You can listen."

Clint sighed and shook his head. He wouldn't be able to convince Dave to not act like an idiot where these kinds were concerned. He'd wait for the call.

It wasn't more than an hour before his phone buzzed. Dave's number was on the ID screen. He answered, but didn't say anything.

"... you're watching me out here in the middle of nowhere. What do you want? Ever occur to you to ask me?'

Fainter: "We're only looking for some people. They were with you when you came. They were working for our boss and stole some things when they left."

"Mendez and the Russian and the Irish? They went to Kylvania. They know someone there. It's where no one can hope to get into."

"Kylvania?"

"A little private country in the middle of the Atlantic off Brazil or somewhere like that."

"But ... how...? We didn't have ... this is crazy!"

Another voice: "Did they leave anything with you? Any papers? Pictures?"

"Pictures? That drug lord or something? I couldn't care less. Why would they leave them with ... so you work for some big shit drug lord and they took some things that could tie his ass to a lamp post?

"They wouldn't leave anything like that with me. I couldn't care less."

"Will you tell, uh, Pablo about it?"

"Who in hell is Pablo? Escobar? Isn't he dead?"

"No. Another Pablo. I can call him. I want to get back to Colombia. This is stupid!

"Please don't tell him I said that!"

There was nothing but background noise for half a minute, then the second voice: "Dr. Goerher? Is, uh *Pablo* there?"

"Can you speak for him? We are with that man in The Darien in Panamá?"

"What? Hello? You are breaking up. There is a bad signal."

Dave: "I have a satellite phone. What's the number. I'll call him. This shit has to stop! I'm in the middle of a goddamned tropical jungle and you follow me around? This shit has to stop!"

Second voice: "Uh, Doctor?"

"Okay."

"I'll punch the number. You will speak with Dr. Goerher, a scientist who works for, uh, Pablo."

There was silence and beeps, then, "Yes? Cardo?"

"Dr. Goerher? This will be the man."

"Dave here. What the hell is this about? Why am I being harassed by two damned Indios from Colombia in the middle of The Darien, for god's sake?"

"Yes. You are the person who they call Dave?" The accent was definitely German.

"Seeing it's my name, yeah. What do you want?"

"The men who were with you earlier. They are no longer there?"

"They went to Kylvania. They weren't very good

in the jungle."

"Kylvania?"

"A private country. Islands. Out from Brazil, I think."

"I am ... not on the computer?"

"Registered through the OAS about twenty five or thirty years ago."

"Hmm. Here it is. Crane? Kiley?"

"Yeah. JK. He's the king."

"Can you give the things they left with you to Cardo? It is things they stole from my part ... boss."

"I told Cardo. They wouldn't leave anything with me. I couldn't care less about some drug lord in Colombia. All they did was show me some pictures of when he was a lot younger or something incoherent. I told them to stick the pictures and their hotshit drug lord up their asses! I'm not impressed with drug lords."

"Could you tell me how they got out of The Darien without being detected?"

"I don't know. They called somebody who had a helicopter pick them up. I was already gone so I don't know if that's what they did. That Viktor ass did say something about a decoy, but I wasn't paying them any attention. I'm here to classify plants. I couldn't care less. All I want is for you people to take this stupid crap somewhere where somebody gives a shit. Leave me the hell alone!"

"Could you allow Cardo to speak with me a moment? I assure you you will no longer be molested. It was from bad information."

Voice two: "Yes?"

"Go to Cartagena. I'll find where this Kylvania is. Maybe you can go there.

"How long before you can get back to what passes for civilization?"

"Two days. We're near a river and can get to somewhere. I'll call."

Silence, then Dave's voice: "Have a safe trip back. You can go up the river to Paya in about ten hours walking. It's not bad.

"I'm getting back to my studies."

"You weren't worried about meeting us here alone?" Voice one asked.

"No. Reno!"

A little background noise. "This is Reno. He's had you in the sights of that pistol since I got here."

A laugh. "You're pretty savvy for a gringo."

"It's why I'm still alive."

"We'll go. You're very boring to watch."

Sounds, then, "Oh, well. Come on, Reno. Let's get back to that big *Cattleya*. I think it'll be *trianaei*, but maybe another labiate. None of them are supposed to be anywhere near here." The phone turned off.

Clint smirked and called JK on the special phone. "They're going to look for Kylvania. Maybe you'll have two Indio guests."

"Okay. How's things?"

"Looking up." They chatted a bit, then Clint went to call Pancho in. They were about ready to head for Quebrada Tula. When Pancho came in he told him about the jungle encounter.

"Echevaria is somewhat powerful. He controls a lot of money. I think it will prove interesting to see if they can get to Kylvania."

"JK will invite them in. They'll find that their quarry has already gone. To Cuba, maybe, or Mexico City. Maybe Los Angeles, but it could be Chicago or New York or Miami or Canberra or London or Paris. Maybe Hong Kong."

"Yes. JK can be as disinterested as Dave. He's not impressed with those bigshit drug lords or their bought-at-auction politicians."

Clint's regular cell phone buzzed. It was from a Private number.

He shrugged and answered.

"Mr. Faraday? I am Dr. Goerher, who I'm sure you've heard of. I was recently speaking with a man they simply call Dave, a botanist. He is in The Darien. He introduced you to three men who you arranged to have removed from The Darien by a helicopter owned by Pedro Quinton.

"You don't know the true story about them, I think. I have shown Dave the proof of what they are up to and he said to contact you. You would know where they are. They possibly left some of the fake evidence with you."

"You talked to Dave? Out there?"

"How else would I know the rest of it?"

"I'm a detective. I don't care about those people (He decided to use Dave's approach). They had some pictures of a drug lord when he was younger or something. They were running from him. They said they have a lot of evidence about something or other. Evidence about drug lords is evidence that will be lost and forgotten anyhow. I don't have the time to waste. I dropped them off in La Palma. They said they knew some king or something as silly. He would take care of them.

"I don't have anything from them. If I did, who pays any attention to that kind of shit anyhow? It's evidence of nothing so far as I'm concerned.

"Oh! It was King JK – they call a king by his initials? – in a place called Kelviniana or something."

"Oh. Well ... thank you. I suppose it's true that no one pays attention to evidence about drug lords. As you say, it would all be lost before it got to the courts or anywhere."

"In the detective business you learn that first thing. Detecting one oh one."

They said goodbyes and hung up.

"Funny! I didn't hear his voice at all and he explained that it was all false to Dave, who fell for it!"

Pancho laughed. "He'll have no choice but to go to Kylvania. I will call JK and suggest a few things. If he goes in person JK will be most interested in trading science with the person who has virtual immortality in his hands!"

"I don't know. All the others who might have seen the evidence weren't interested and thought it was all science fiction or something."

"Life's a bitch."

They joked as they packed their things in Clint's boat and headed for Quebrada Tula. They would take the boat up the Rio Guarinaro as far as they could toward Quebrada Tula. Clint had friends in a little settlement there who would watch his boat and would take him to the town in cayucas. They would take horses from Quebrada Tula into the mountains where he had his second home.

They arrived at the house to find it occupied by a young man. He was staying there because no one was there so he could keep it in good repair. He would go.

Clint said there was no reason for him to go. They would be here a few days, then go back.

Clint talked to him in dialect. It wasn't quite right. It would seem Echevaria *did* find a way to get someone there.

Clint acted like he was unsuspicious. He waited until Tino slipped out the back and went around. He would definitely watch the door, so Clint wouldn't come from the door being watched.

Tino took out a satellite phone and punched a number. He spoke with a Yvan, then was passed to Echevaria. He said Clint only had someone named Pancho with him. What was he to do now? Clint said he could stay.

There was a pause. Tino said he didn't know. A Pancho with a wife named Gloria and a daughter named Serena.

Tino was suddenly very nervous. He looked at the house and started almost running down the narrow path toward Quebrada Tula.

Clint took a little shortcut and stepped out in front of Tino with a pistol pointed right at him. He pointed to the phone and held out his hand for it.

"Echevaria? This is Clint Faraday. This has gone far enough. You've sold your soul to the devil. You are not to involve anyone else in this or I'm going to destroy you.

"I didn't learn anything from this man. I knew

all about you and Goerher before I came here. I hoped you would have sense enough to get away from it here. Nobody cares. Nobody wants life extension."

"Mr. Faraday? This is Goerher. Echevaria is no longer in the room. You are a problem, I think. You know. If you know, others know.

"Is it true that Francisco DeGulio is there with you?"

"Pancho? Yes."

"Echevaria is terrified. He says DeGulio can have the army come here with a word."

"He can, but probably not the Colombian army. The armies of every other drug lord in Colombia and Peru, though.

"Just drop it! Go back to Colombia and stay there. Nobody will bother you if you don't do anything more. You passed the line when you killed that kid!"

"I did not do that! I swear, it was Echevaria! I would not allow that kind of thing, but it is what he knows."

"Sharky?"

There was a pause. "Yes. That was my orders. He and the other three have stolen my research."

"They have some pictures and a story, not the research."

"They have some pictures and a story. That is

what the story is. They have my research on computer chips! It will not be in my control if they get it out. They are not the kind of people who deserve the process! Do you know what will happen when every sordid little tin king can live for hundreds of years?

"It must be kept secure. They will sell it for money to anyone! Echevaria is one of them. I sold it for money to continue the research, but was able to control him with the threat of withdrawing the process. He has become what he was. He is stupid. He spends all his time doing what he did when he was younger. Women, women, women. He thinks of nothing else except making money in any way he can, no matter how sick and twisted!"

"I'll see that the research isn't there for anyone. I can do that a lot easier than you'd believe. You stay completely out of it. Get all your people out of this country!

"Understand one thing! If you've lied to me – about anything – you're done! As a friend said, life extension won't stop a bullet through your head!"

"Something I have considered where Echevaria is concerned. Done."

Clint handed the phone back for Tino to be told he was to come back to Colombia. Clint went to the house to get his own satellite phone. The special one. He called JK and told him what was going on. Pancho was there and spoke for a moment with JK. When he finished he said, "Clint, there will be a helicopter here very soon. You and I are going to Kylvania to speak with your innocents."

"Pedro can get here fast. We can be ready. I don't know if he has the range to get to Kylvania. I don't know where it is."

"JK is sending the chopper. It is faster than anything anyone else has. It has the range to make Europe."

"JK knows the coordinates?"

"It would be to the GPS numbers of your phone when you spoke with him a moment ago. He has that information instantly without regard to which phone is used."

They went inside and packed enough for two days and were just going outside again when the chopper came. They got aboard and were off!

Clint hadn't known there was a chopper that could move nearly that fast or go nearly that high!

Kylvania was a half dozen large islands and numerous small ones in the ocean off the Guianas. They were in a band that got little rain and were ignored for that for years. JK had a special unit that made very pure water from sea water and the islands were now lush. Dave had brought thousands of orchids, bromelliads and other things and had put in an irrigation system that was automatic.

JK was a thin man in his early thirties. He had a habit of wandering off in the middle of a conversation when he got an idea. He was a genius.

"Well, JK! This is Clint!" Pancho introduced. "I see Dave has been here since I was last."

"He brought another couple of thousand plants. Birdbeak is now the most complete tropical epiphytic plant research garden in the world! He has a few students living there with the top three experts in the world as professors. The students are all Indians from Central America.

"You know how he is about education. He already has two students who graduated from here in the top ten in the world at an age where the other eight are three times their age!

"I have all the information you suggested. They really did have all that information, including a few videos on chips and memory sticks. Most of it is on four and six gig chips. Goerher is a true genius. I can't actually argue with his ideas of Malthusian limits. I've said the world was more than double overpopulated for years."

"You said 'Did have?' Not have?" Pancho asked.

"Their crap had some kind of freak accident. It jumbled all the info."

"How did you find it?" Clint asked.

"It's patterned. I can induce a mini-current that makes it show a blip on a screen. They were exhausted when they arrived and went to bed after a very good meal. So far as they know everything was exactly the way it was when they went to sleep."

Pancho nodded. Clint started to say something, then grinned.

"He's the king here. The law here is as different from the US as the Panamanian law is from the comarcas," Pancho said.

"You can do what needs to be done when other are at risk. My law doesn't have a lot of stupid technicalities that protect criminals and you can hardly bribe me when I can sit at any comp in any internet café and have half the money in the world in a personal bank account that can't be checked.

"It's your show. What now?"

"Did you preserve the method?" Clint asked.

"Obviously. What law have they exceeded to mean they are deported?"

"Let me make a call," Clint suggested. "I can get a declaration that they are no longer sought for anything so they can't claim amnesty here?"

"Go for it!"

Clint called Goerher. "Clint Faraday here. The evidence spoken of earlier no longer exists. I am in Kylvania. They had the chips you spoke of. Those chips had some kind of freak accident that erased them." He raised an eyebrow at JK. JK held his hand out for the phone.

"JK here. There was a freak ion display as they came onto the island. As you know, unshielded electronic storage can become jumbled from such things. They were in the air without any natural shielding.

"Dr. Goerher, your research is brilliant. I agree that it should not be made available to more than ninety nine point nine percent of the people alive right now. I also agree with Clint and his chief that those are exactly the percent who would refuse the process.

"For the research it is worthwhile and brilliant. For practicality it is of no use at this time.

"Perhaps we can work together? You can come to Kylvania. This should be completed and advanced in the hope that someday it will be useful. It already was in one instance. It allowed you the time to make it a workable thing."

"I would very much like to be with someone who is more than a beaker of concentrated greed. I will listen to any proposal you may have, not including that you have the process used on yourself. Should you prove worthy it will be automatic."

"I might go for some small extension, but very limited. I'm among the ones who would refuse it."

Pancho and Clint went outside while JK talked with Goerher. "This might work out well for many," Pancho said. Clint nodded.

They cleaned up and went around the place, then went for dinner in the big dining room where everyone on the main island went to eat. There weren't many people there. JK had asked that dinner be held an hour later than usual so he would have time to have a special guest appear.

Clint and Pancho were at the table with JK and his wife, a knockout intelligent woman who met him when she was the head model for a Crane electronics company computer promotion. Viktor and Mendez came in and stopped to stare for a second. Clancy came a couple of minutes later and greeted Clint heartily.

JK came in ten or so minutes later with the rather distinguished-looking man from the photos. He introduced Dr. Goerher. Clancy, Mendez and Viktor looked like trapped animals.

"I would like to introduce Dr. Hans Goerher. He is a research scientist in genetics. He will be living here.

"Believe it or not, he is more than a hundred twenty five years old so I won't have to explain his branch of the science.

"Hans has recently – as of this afternoon, as a matter of fact – escaped an impossible situation in Colombia. What and who were behind that is of no concern to us.

"These other three have to do with that. They won't be staying long, so introductions aren't necessary.

"Well! This is Pancho, who some of you have met. This is Clint Faraday, a detective and friend of CD and Alma.

"If this tastes half as good as it smells, the chef gets a raise! Dig in!"

"Thank you," Goerher said. "I wish to say to the three JK mentioned that they are in no danger now. Not from me. If they cause no further bits of distraction they are in no danger from anyone. What they have and what they were hiding from was mostly myth. Knowing how a piano is played, the position of each key, the notes on paper, does not make the clutz a pianist. One must have some ability or the knowledge is for nought. Knowing a procedure and being able to perform that procedure are very different things.

"Your former boss never understood that. It is why he insisted upon pursuing such as you. In doing so he has ascertained that the procedure with him as subject stops. We will see how the reversal affects the results, what?

"I agree! If this tastes a third as good as it smells I will add to the chef's raise!"

They enjoyed a truly gourmet dinner, then went their various ways for the evening. There was a small bar. Clint noted that JK had Flor de Caña rum. It was the only rum available he could say was good.

Clancy came to them after a few minutes. JK had an idea and was in his laboratory. Clint spoke with an Indio student he'd met in Chiriqui Grande, then went to where Pancho was talking with Goerher and Clancy.

"We were just informing Mr. James that he was in no danger except possibly for Echevaria. He claims only Sharky had access to the research and that the other three were only along because Echevaria and I thought they were involved," Goerher said. "I find it amusing. I was about to explain to Mr. James that there is constant surveillance of the computer section Mendez might have made such a claim where we don't have direct and irrefutable evidence that it is not true.

"Be that as it may, I no longer care. They have every detail of the process and no ability to use it. Without a special talent I have through my genetic heritage they cannot hope to make it work.

"I am indebted, in a way, to them! It has led me here and away from a monster with little hint of intelligence. We shall, as I suggested, see how the subject reacts to the process being withdrawn.

"Mr. Faraday, I thank you for making me stop to think. It is true no one who would be eligible for the process is worth the effort.

"Whatever is the matter with Viktor? He is trying, to an extreme, to get your attention, Mr. James. Please inform him that I present no danger to any of you directly."

Clancy turned and went to Viktor, who had a laptop in his hand. He showed the screen to Clancy, who went out. Viktor followed him.

"It would seem that our Mr. Ivanovich has discovered that what little they had is gone!" Goerher said. Clint grinned. Pancho matched the grin.

They didn't see the three before going to bed. Clint had a room across the hall from Pancho. About two in the morning there was a knock on his door. He opened it to find Mendez standing there.

"What?"

"How did you do it? I'll admit we probably couldn't have done it, but we would have found someone who can."

"I don't know what the hell you're talking

about."

"The chips. They're erased."

"Erased? The chips? You mean the research crap?"

"Yes. Not erased, really. Just scrambled. You did it in a way we can't even be sure you moved them. I have a couple of old floppies there and they weren't bothered. How did you do that without erasing any of those things?"

"I wouldn't know how. Maybe JK ... but why would he care? He didn't even know about them, did he?"

He looked thoughtful, then shook his head. JK was just then coming into the hallway (What a coincidence!) and stopped to ask if everything was alright.

"Mendez says his computer chips were erased or scrambled or something. The floppies with them weren't. How could that happen?"

"When?"

"When what?"

"When were they scrambled? Was it while you were between here and the coast?"

"I don't know! Why?"

"Sunspots earlier. On the ground it's nothing serious. If you were in the air and got an ionic blast, it could erase or scramble a sensitive memory. If it didn't erase floppies that were right there, that's what it would have to be. We did have a peak in ionic bombardment about four or ... it was at four oh nine to four eleven.

"What time did you get here? If you were more than five hundred feet here you wouldn't get protection from direct."

"We got here at four fifteen. We would have been over the ocean. It seems our luck sucks lately!"

"Life's like that. Good night, Clint. Mendez."

Mendez sighed. "Good night." He walked off. Clint went back to bed.

Clint stepped off the chopper. He had just taken Pancho and family to the airport where Pancho's private jet would take him back to Florida.

Tyna came out with Nicole. Nito was down by the dock cleaning the fish for dinner.

Pedro waved and left. Clint went toward the house with Tyna and Nicole.

He loved that place. He loved Quebrada Tula. He loved the comarca and the people there. His primary love was of his family.

They went inside. Clint called Dave and caught him up to date, then called JK, who reported the problem seemed to be handled very well. It was wait and see. Goerher was truly brilliant and was working with the students on the genetic end of their schooling.

"He told me about some of the things he did while working with Hitler. He didn't see anything wrong with it at the time. Looking back, he was some kind of science fiction monster. He was not the same person today, thank the gods he didn't believe in.

"Clancy and Viktor are in Germany. Mendez

went to Rio, where he has relatives. I don't know anything about Echevaria. He called Goerher several times, screaming rage at first with a lot of silly threats, then trying to make a deal, now begging. Lucy is to tell him Goerher had burned all his papers and had gone back to Germany. He seemed to be insane to her!

"We'll know if the process wears off fast or medium or slow in about four months. If there's no change, he'll just live the rest of a natural lifespan that had a pause of thirty years in it. If there's a little change, it will be an accelerated aging. If it's a lot, he'll die within three years of old age. If it starts going that fast, it won't stop where he would have been anyhow.

"Anything new with you?"

"Every day! This is truly paradise. The whole comarca is a lot like Dave's gardens on Birdbeak. Fishing is good, the gardens are good, the weather's good, life's good."

They chatted a bit, then rung off. Clint sighed happily and went down to talk with his son at the dock.

"I hear you spent the last few nights with Don Juan," Clint said. "Do they call him that because he's a young pussyhound?"

"Yeah. He likes sex. We did things I've never done. It was fun, but I think I'm not much for the gay stuff. I would rather be with Chacha, but she's going to school in Chiriqui Grande. Maybe Linda and Flora can keep me happy, huh?"

"If I wasn't so horny all the time at your age, I'd probably act like a gringo father now and give you a lecture about how you were ruining your life, but that's bullshit and you know it! Just be careful. I won't have you knocking some girl up and running away without the responsibility. This family doesn't do things like that."

"Dave gave me some stuff that's a hundred percent. I won't knock anybody up."

They talked about sex a bit, then Clint went back to the house. He thought how strange that conversation would be to most in the states and grinned. It was good to be here!

It had been five months. Echevaria was aging normally so would have the forty years taken off added to his natural lifespan. He did seem borderline insane, but Goerher said he was never very stable. He hoped the mind didn't suddenly go from the process.

Pancho called two days later. Echevaria had acted like the early days of the drug cartels and had gotten into a gunfight with a rival cartel. He was history, so they would never know if the process would change things in ways they didn't yet know if it was halted.

He sighed. Why couldn't people accept that there was a natural span for most things, that few were prepared for extensions of some things.

Goerher was an exception. He also admitted that should he grow bored with life he had no problem with ending it.

Clint thought Goerher would be a lot like Dave. As long as there was research to be done with the plants he would be content with his life. If something happened that would mean he sat in a rocking chair to wait for death he'd make it a short wait!

Clint thought things were just about right. He wasn't the type to ever become bedridden. He was going to enjoy the rest of his life. So far, his was charmed.

Well, tomorrow, fishing with Omar!

C. D. Moulton's works are available on most major outlets as printed or e-books. CD writes the CD Grimes, PI, mysteries, the Det. Lt. Nick Storie mysteries, the Clint Faraday mysteries, the Flight of the Maita science fiction series, books on orchid culture and many others of many types. Mystery, adventure, intrigue, science fiction, humor, fantasy, paranormal, mild erotica, and factual.

www.ingramcontent.com/pod-product-compliance
Lightning Source LLC
Chambersburg PA
CBHW072205150726
48002CB00014B/1308